Best Bible
STORIES

DANGER ON THE LONELY ROAD

Jennifer Rees Larcombe
Illustrated by Steve Björkman

Marshall Pickering
An Imprint of HarperCollins*Publishers*

Marshall Pickering is an Imprint of
HarperCollins*Religious*
Part of HarperCollins*Publishers*
77–85 Fulham Palace Road
London W6 8JB

First published in 1992 in Great Britain
by Marshall Pickering as part of
Children's Bible Story Book by Jennifer Rees Larcombe
This edition published in 1999 by Marshall Pickering

1 3 5 7 9 10 8 6 4 2

Text Copyright © 1992, 1999 Jennifer Rees Larcombe
Illustrations Copyright © 1999 Steve Björkman

Jennifer Rees Larcombe and Steve Björkman assert the moral right to be
identified as the author and illustrator of this work

A catalogue record for this book is
available from the British Library

ISBN 0 551 03228 6

Printed and bound in Hong Kong

DANGER ON THE LONELY ROAD

'Go and arrest this Jesus,'

the Pharisees told the temple police.
'We can't have everyone in Jerusalem thinking
he's the
Messiah!'

But those policemen made a
big mistake.

They stopped and **listened** to
what Jesus was saying.

'Love people who hate you. Be kind to people who do mean things to you.'

The policemen stood with their mouths open. 'God's rules say we must love God and other people as much as we love ourselves,' said one of the Pharisees, trying to trick Jesus with a difficult question. 'But surely a good Jew can only love good people?'

'I'll tell you a story that will answer that,' said Jesus, as everyone gathered eagerly round him.

'Once a man was travelling **alone** between Jerusalem and Jericho.'

'Agh!' gasped the crowd. They all knew what a lonely, dangerous road that was. It wound between towering rocks, where robbers lurked in the dark shadows, waiting to pounce. Everyone hated to be **alone** on that road.

'Suddenly,' continued Jesus, 'out jumped a gang of ragged men armed with sticks and knives. They **seized** his money, **beat** him cruelly and ran away, leaving him **bleeding** on the ground.

Not long afterwards a priest walked by on his way to the temple in Jerusalem.

"Tut, tut," he said when he saw the man lying there covered in blood and flies.

"Poor man. But if I stop to help, I'll spoil my temple clothes."

So he hurried on past.

The injured man lay longing for someone to come. At last he heard footsteps, and round the corner came a Pharisee. "He spends his life telling people about God's rules," he thought.

"Surely he'll help."

Nervously the Pharisee crept over and peered down at the wounded man. "Suppose the robbers who attacked this man are still hiding here," he shivered.

"They'll probably hurt me too and steal my money." He disappeared into the distance.
"No one will come now," thought the man. "It's beginning to get dark and by morning I'll be dead."

It was then that he heard the "clop, clop"

of a donkey's hooves, but his heart **sank**
when he opened his eyes.

It was **only a Samaritan.**

He certainly wouldn't help. (The Samaritans and
the Jews were such enemies they wouldn't even
speak to each other.)

How astonished he was when he felt **kind** hands lifting his head. Someone was giving him a drink and rubbing soothing ointment into his painful cuts.

Strong arms lifted him onto a donkey and took him all the way to a hotel.

"Why is this Samaritan being so kind?" he wondered when he found himself lying in a clean, comfortable bed.

"They stole all my money," he managed to say.

"Don't worry," smiled the Samaritan. "You can stay here until you're better;

I'm paying the bill for you.'"

Jesus looked round at the crowd.

'Which man in that story really loved the injured man?' he asked. 'Was it the good Jew who always kept the rules?' 'No,' said the Pharisee uncomfortably.

'It was the Samaritan.'

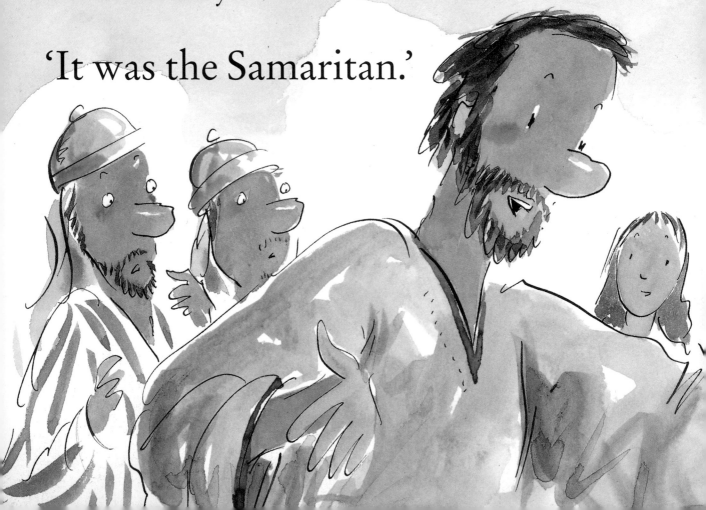

'Then you go and
love
people like that too,'

said Jesus.

'Well, where is he?' demanded the Pharisees when the policemen came back without Jesus.

Looking very **embarrassed,** the policemen replied,

'We never heard anyone talking like this before.'

Luke 10:25-37